GRANDMA MATTIE GOES TO CHURCH

SARAH TUCK

Sarah Tuck Books for adults/18-years and older Readers/Authorship:

Play Manufactured in United States of America

Second Edition

Library of Congress in Publication Data

ISBN 9780578474083 (paperback)

ISBN 9780578484525 (e-book)

 Created with Vellum

GRANDMA MATTIE GOES TO CHURCH WITH MR. WASHINGTON

Tina can't wait to get home with her best friend Samantha to share with her the latest of what's been going on with Mr. Washington and Grandma Mattie in how they enjoyed the backyard party yesterday. She is so excited she can hardly wait.

She gets home and goes into the bedroom and changes; while Samantha goes to the bathroom to wash up so that she can warm up the food and fix her a plate. Then Tina heads for the kitchen to wash her hands and she fixes her a plate and she go into the living room and starts talking and eating.

"Well I guess that you are wondering why I asked you over here after church today." Samantha was coming out of the kitchen with a large bowl of Spaghetti, French toast and salad. She loved eating at Tina house on Sunday after church she always knew that on this day she didn't have to cook at home.

Yes, don't tell me that Grandma Mattie and Mr. Washington aren't working out, Samantha said.

Tina looked over at her with a smile on her face and said no they are really hitting it off real good girl. As a matter of fact he had such a good time at the party and with Grandma Mattie. Why now he wants all of us to come to his church in October for their pastor Anniversary.

Samantha stopped eating and looked around with a surprised look on her face and then she took a sip of the tall glass of lemonade that she had been drinking and said. "Why girl that sounds good, are you going?"

Tina had just put a bite of her salad into her mouth when she held up her finger to tell Samantha to wait a minute and let me chew this up first and then I will answer you.

"Yes I am and you were invited too," Tina replied. You know that you are just like family too.

Samantha started laughing and looked over at Tina with a gaze in her eyes. She knew that she had always been treated like she was a member of the family and she was so happy that she had been invited too. It was nothing like being around Tina family when I wasn't with mines.

Oh ok, well I had better let mom know that I want be at our church on that Sunday, because if I don't go, she will be calling me and asking me where I was. Samantha said. Girl this calls for me to get me a new outfit now, I want to look my best on that Sunday.

Tina then spoke up and said; I know what you mean girl. Samantha had just taken another drink of her Lemonade and sat her glass back down on the table. Then she looked over at Tina and said, yeah I'm in my 30's now and she still treats me like I'm her little girl.

Tina just laughed and finished eating; and then leaned back on the couch and said: Mom is kind of the same way. I guess that we will always be their little girl no matter how old we get.

Samantha turned and looked at Tina again and said; "I guess so, Samantha was almost finished with her food when she said with some excitement in her voice, you know what?" I was just thinking.

Tina was rubbing her stomach because she was full from that good meal that she had cooked early that morning for them to eat. She would have had the leftovers from the backyard party that they had yesterday; but since a lot of the family wanted to take a plate home from the cook-out. There wasn't enough left. What were you thinking about? Tina replied.

Samantha started smiling and clapping her hands and eased out to the edge of the couch and said; we might get lucky girl and find us a good man at this church. One of those good church going men that carries his Bible with him most of the time.

Tina rolled her head around like that girl on the Exodus; you wouldn't believe the look that she gave her; why that look could kill, and then she said with a smart attitude; you said that right, we might get lucky.

Aw now it was on, Samantha was laughing so hard that she had turned red in the face. Yes she was one of those light skinned chic's that when her emotions showed; you could always see the impression on her face. Samantha replied back to her and said; well you know that old saying. There are a lot of good men in church like there, are a lot of good women.

"Yeah I know that's what they say and I'm sure there are, but I haven't had any luck." Tina said.

Then she began to thank about the aches and pains that she had in the last few years and blurted out; why I can see me now trying to have a man this day and time is going to be a little difficult for me. Samantha said why do you say that Tina?

Well, that's because I used to go to bed smelling like Victoria Secret and know I go to bed smelling like Ben Gay. They both started laughing so hard there were tears in their eyes.

At that very moment the doorbell rang and Tina could see through the door that it was Ms. Hattie Mae, one of the nosey twin sisters. So she said get down; they try to hide so that she couldn't see them; but by Tina having a glass front door; she could still see them thru the door.

Samantha then spoke up and said; do you think that she seen us? Tina replied and said I don't know just stay down. They were laughing and giggling while they were down there on their knees trying to hide from her.

Ms. Hattie Mae wasn't going anywhere so she continued to peep thru the glass door to see if she could see anyone inside. Then she said I see you'll in there; come open this door she said. Tina then gets up and goes to the door and lets her in. She says, why come in Ms. Hattie Mae, you have to excuse us we were looking for an earring that fell on the floor.

Ms. Hattie Mae said why thank you for letting me in, well did you find it?

Tina replied and said, no ma'am we didn't but we will look for it a little later. What brings you over this way? Why I just happen to be in the neighborhood and I thought that I would come over to see how you were doing she said. Then she looked over at Samantha and said; Oh hi Samantha.

"Samantha looked over at her and then she looked her up and down and then said hi Ms. Hattie Mae".

Tina was puzzled why Ms Hattie Mae was way over on this side of town. So she spoke up and said, so you just happen to be in the neighborhood you say.

Ms. Hattie Mae had just gotten comfortable and sat her purse over on the table; then she turned and looked at Tina and said; yes, and I was wondering how Grandma Mattie and her new man was doing she said. Tina eyebrow went up and she had the funniest look on her face.

And the reason why she had this funny look on her face was because she lived right next door to Grandma Mattie. So what puzzled her was why would she drive all the way over on this side of town to want to find out how she and Mr. Washington was doing. When she could have just stepped next door and talk to her one on one and then she would have know how she was doing.

She then said I see, well they are doing very well thank you; then Ms. Hattie Mae smiled and said that is nice to hear, I had been thinking about them and I wanted to know if you could tell me, how long have they been going together?

"Samantha then turned and looked at Mrs. Hattie Mae and she wasn't smiling either."

Samantha couldn't believe that Mrs. Hattie had the nerve to be asking about Grandma Mattie and her man already when their relationship was still fresh. Samantha shook her head and turned and looked at her right in her eyes and said why Mrs. Hattie Mae you are full of surprises today. I'm sure that you have gathered by now that Ms. Hattie Mae didn't quiet care for Samantha. Nor did Samantha care for her.

However, the both of them always tried to be cordial to each other; and to be honest I really don't think that either one of them knows why they really don't care for each other.

Tina then turned and touched Samantha arm and said I got this, Ok. Now, Ms. Hattie Mae, I know you mean well and all, but I don't know what you got in mind. But it's not going to happen. You see Grandma Mattie is happy and I'm going to make sure that she stays that way. Ms. Hattie Mae said well of course, I want the same thing that you do.

"Samantha looked over at her and said I'm sure you do and rolled her eyes."

Ms. Hattie Mae moved around in her seat and looked at the both of them and said I was just checking to see how things were going with them and to let you know that he is really a nice looking man. You know he looks like somebody that I may have seen before.

Tina turned and looked at her and without waiting another minute and said is that right. Please feel free to tell me more. Tina was interested in hearing how she knew Mr. Washington; cause if she had known him personally. She knew that there was going to be a problem.

Ms. Hattie Mae spoke up and said well you know me I'm always going here and there when there is something going on. So I just might have seen him when I was out somewhere that's all I was going to say.

She was always traveling from place to place and she did have some pictures, to prove that she had gone to some of those places that she was always talking about thru the years.

Tina had a sign of relief and said ok Mrs. Hattie Mae if you say that's all it is to this.

"Why yes it is, then she looked at Tina with a surprised look and said, oh now you are not thinking that I'm over here after him do you?" Ms. Hattie Mae said. Samantha couldn't wait to jump in and give her a piece of her mind; so she turned and looked at her and said that's exactly what she is thinking.

Ms. Hattie Mae looked around at her with another surprising look on her face and said what? Tina could see that she was shocked in what Samantha had told her so she tried to smooth it over by saying; well what she is trying to say is that you know a lot of people. So that would explain why you are asking.

Oh ok, she said and you are absolutely right. Why I love going places and meeting different people. This is why I'm so well know around here and a few other places.

Then she said well I guess I had better be going. I've got a lot of things I need to do today.

Tina then stood up and said well alright Ms. Hattie Mae and I wanted to thank you for stopping by and I will make sure to let Grandma Mattie know that you asked about her and Mr. Washington Tina said.

Then as Ms. Hattie Mae was getting up and getting ready to leave she turned to Tina and said well you make sure that you do that Tina. Then she looked over at Samantha and said, oh and bye Samantha. Samantha then looked right back and said Bye!!!

Tina then walks her to the door and says bye and then she turns and comes right back and into the living room and sat down on the couch.

Samantha looked out the door and waited till she seen her go by the window and down the steps and get into her car and leave and then she leaned back on the couch looked over at Tina and said what was that all about?

Oh she was just being noisy, you know that Grandma Mattie is always saying that her and Ms. Ida Mae is always popping up every time that we have something. Why they think that they are part of the family now.

Yes they do said Samantha, but if I'm thinking right, I think that she is trying to take Mr. Washington away from Grandma Mattie.

Tina turned and looked at her with a strange look and replied and said I'm not worried about that, because Grandma Mattie can handle her own.

Samantha said yes she can but I'm just surprised in what all Ms. Hattie Mae had to say. Yes she was full of surprises today Tina said. As usual she has always wanted to snoop around in other people business. Anyway we had better get back to what we were talking about.

Samantha grinned and said alright; well I know that you have heard Mrs. Margie and Grandma Mattie say someone will come when you least expect them too.

At this particular time Tina mind started wondering back to what her Grandma Mattie had told her. Then she remembered at that very moment what her mom had told her as well. Yes I have, and I'm still praying for that someone. Tina said.

Samantha could see that Tina was a little bit sad when she mentioned her mother. So she went on to say; well I am too, I'm excited though and I'm looking forward to going with you.

"Ok then, well I had better check with Uncle Jessie to make sure that his suit is clean; and I guess he will have to stay with me on that Saturday night to make sure that he doesn't get messed up." Tina said. I would hate to see him going to church and stumbling through the door with liquor on his breath.

Samantha replied back and said; that sounds like a good idea to me. Tina took a deep breath and said; yes it does. Besides I don't want to let Grandma Mattie down because after all I wouldn't want anything causing a problem between them two.

While taking her shoes off to rest her feet, she then turned to Tina and said I was really surprised in how Uncle Jessie was on his best behavior at the cook-out.

Tina looked at her and said he tried to act up, but like I told him. It wasn't that kind of party, and I had a few people to help me keep him from putting liquor into the punch bowl. For some strange reason every since Uncle Jessie and Aunt Pauline broke up. He's been drowning his self in that bottle.

Samantha was drinking lemonade and she almost got strangled, she coughed a few times and wiped her chin and said a women like that will make you take a drink or two. Shoot I never knew how to take her. One minute she was sweet as she could be. And the next time you seen her she was ready to bit your head off.

Tina then said well Uncle Jessie wasn't always an angel himself. Why he put her through a lot of things I heard when I was coming up. And now I think that he has finally realized that she was the best thing that every happen to him. That's why you always see him with a bottle in his hand. Trying to drink his self to death I guess.

As the old saying goes as always, it takes them to hit rock bottom to figure it all out said Samantha; Tina just shrugged her shoulder and said I know that's right. Then they want to come crawling back to you. You said that right Tina said.

While Samantha was still sitting there looking at the television, all she could think about was how she and Tina was going to be able to find them some good men going to this church.

Samantha then spoke up and said; I still say that we are going to get lucky on that day. Girl I just can't wait; why I can just see it, now you know I'm like Grandma Mattie I like my man tall and full of life. And for you, let's just say that you are going to meet the man of your dreams.

"Then Tina spoke up and said; Samantha stop dreaming and they both laughed. Samantha then picked up the television control and started scrolling throug the different channels trying to find a good movie for them to watch.

2

IT'S THE 1ST OF THE MONTH THE LADIES MEET WITH GRANDMA MATTIE

It's that time of the month when Grandma Mattie and the ladies from the church have their monthly meeting at the restaurant. Everyone is coming in one by one smiling and greeting each other then they sat down to start eating after going through the buffet line.

While they have all been seated and they were gathered around the table eating and laughing; then suddenly here comes Grandma Mattie running in a little late; she's smiling as well, but the ladies notice something different about her. She is wearing a red dress with silver jewelry, black pumps and a matching purse and she even had a hat on that matched her dress then she takes her seat.

"Well hello Grandma Mattie; well aren't you glowing today with your pretty red dress on." Sister Viola said.

Sister Viola was a soft spoken lady with a medium frame with gray hair; she wore glasses and she was a little on the plump side most of the time she would always complained about her knees hurting her. This was one of Sister Mattie friends of the church. She wore a pink dress with a matching pink pearl necklace and matching earrings; she wore the prettiest makeup that accented her dress.

"Yes I must say that you are looking rather nice today." We've been missing you lately. Sister Pauline said. Hope that all is well with you and the family.

Sister Pauline was Grandma Mattie daughter in law; she had married her son Jessie. She was also a medium frame lady with a cute short cut curly hair style and she wore glasses too. You had to know her to appreciate her, because she would say some of the strange things that you would ever want to hear.

She wore a black dress that day with a matching black hat. She had on white pearl earrings and necklace.

Grandma Mattie just smiled and looked over at her and said; why thank you Pauline, it's nothing special; just something I pulled out of the closet; and I've been a little busy lately. Oh and the family is doing well thank you.

"I'm sorry that we started eating without you we thought that you weren't coming again today." Sister Viola said. That's quiet alright, I wouldn't want you all to sit and wait on little old me.

Well I have left a few messages but you hadn't returned any of them. That's when Grandma Mattie spoke up and said well I've been sort of busy then she smiled. I had been meaning to call you but I just didn't get around to it. Please forgive me. No worries said Sister Viola.

Then out of no were Sister Ida Mae turned and looked at Grandma Mattie and said; why don't you want to tell them the good news Grandma Mattie, why you are glowing and have that great big smile on your face? She said. You see Sister Ida Mae was a twin sister of Hattie Mae; and they both lived next door to Grandma Mattie. They had been neighbors for years. Grandma Mattie always wondered why the two of them never had gotten married. Until one day she found out how nosey they were. That explained why they had never gotten married.

Grandma Mattie looked up from eating her food and replied and said now there she goes dipping all in my Kool-Aid.

"Yes Grandma Mattie, tell them; I'm sure that they would want to know," said Sister Hattie Mae.

Sister Hattie Mattie was a tall thick lady with short sandy and black hair and she had gold in her mouth; she was a lady that always liked to dress sharp in her matching shoes and purse. She too was a busybody and was always going here and there.

Grandma Mattie turned around and looked at her and shook her head; then she said under her breath, I can see right now that I'm going to have to put up a taller fence; them women are so nosey; they don't know how to stay out of other people business. They are always meddling.

What's going on with you Grandma Mattie? What are they talking about? Sister Viola said.

Grandma Mattie felt like she was being ambushed and she felt like she needed to spell the tea and let them know what was going on with her. So she spoke up and said; well I wasn't going to say anything; but I guess I can tell you all the good news. Well my granddaughter Tina, you all know Tina. They all shook their heads and said yes. Well she fixed me up on a blind date and his name is Mr. Berry Washington and we have been going out now for a little while now.

Sister Pauline stopped eating and turned and looked at Grandma Mattie and said; ''so that explains why you haven't been showing up for bunch and some of our meetings.

Then here comes one of the nosey twin sisters Ida Mae speaking up and says; you should have been at the backyard Party. It was just lovely and I had a ball.

Sister Pauline then looks over to Grandma Mattie with a surprised look on her face and said; Backyard Party, why what is she talking about Grandma Mattie.

Grandma Mattie almost choked on the food that she had put in her mouth; so she took a sip of her tea cleared her throat, wiped her mouth and then replied and said; oh it's nothing really. Tina just had some of our family over and a few of our friends for the Backyard Party on the 4th of July to meet Mr. Washington that's all. I'm sorry that she forgot to invite you, Sister Pauline.

Sister Pauline said Um that was alright because I was busy canning my pickles and I wouldn't have been able to come anyway.

Sister Viola couldn't stay still in her seat and she was so anxious to get in on this conversation; she could hardly wait so she stopped eating and looked over to Grandma Mattie and said; when are we going to meet this Mr. Berry Washington?

"Oh you will get to meet him soon enough, maybe when he comes to church with me." Grandma Mattie said.

Sister Pauline looked over at Grandma Mattie and said; church, what kind of man you got. She was always speaking up and saying things before she thought about speaking. And without hesitation she had went and done it again.

Sis Viola was shocked to hear Sister Pauline speaking like that so she turned and looked over her glasses at her and spoke up and said; why Sister Pauline.

If you could have seen the look on Sister Pauline face, you would have cracked up. She was clueless in what she had said. Then she came back with saying oh I'm sorry, what I meant to say was; how did you get him to want to go to church with you?

Grandma Mattie then spoke up and said, it wasn't that hard, why I just ask him would he like to go to church with me sometimes and then he said that he would and later he asked me if I would attend church with him sometimes that's all.

"So that's all you did huh, well I used to try to get Jessie to go to church for fifteen years: and all he would say to me is he wasn't ready yet; or that he didn't have anything to wear."

Grandma Mattie looked over at Pauline and smiled and said; I know he's my son and he has had his issues. But I'm still praying for the both of you and I know that God is going to answer my prayers one of these days.

Then Sister Viola started thinking about her late husband James right about then; and then she spoke up and said; well at least the two of you have a man; I'm still looking for one.

Sister Pauline didn't waste any time jumping in and saying, "Correction, I used to have a man, remember we've been separated for three years now or have you all forgotten it.

Grandma Mattie folded her hands and sat back in her chair and looked over at Sister Viola and said; looking for one, Viola how long have you been going to church?

Sister Viola didn't waste any time in answering her and said why ever since I was a little girl. Then Grandma Mattie said and how long has James been passed? She thought for a little bit and then she answered said about seven years now. Sister Viola replied.

Grandma Mattie was older than the rest of the sister sitting there and she had more wisdom and knowledge than all of them. And by her father being a minister she knew her Bible like the back of her hand. So she looked at Sister Viola and said, now you know what the Bible says, Proverbs 18 – 22, a man who fines a wife finds a good thing. So you stop looking for a man right now. Then she asked her if she had been praying.

Grandma Mattie used to sing in the choir when she was younger; her father used to love to hear her sing. This is where she inherited some of her wisdom and knowledge and from her mother. Her mother was a nurse and she was the director of the choir and she could sing too.

Why yes I have and I thought that I had someone; he took me out a few times and on our third date he wanted to collect and I was very upset with him and I asked him to leave.

"Poor Sister Pauline hadn't caught onto the conversation yet so she speaks up and says;" Collect what?

Grandma Mattie just starts shaking her head and looked over at Sister Pauline and said; now I see why Jessie married you. Then Grandma Mattie spoke up and said; Sister Pauline she's talking about he was ready to make his self feel at home.

Sister Pauline was sitting there again trying to figure out what going on. She lifted her hands and raised them up one by one as she said collect, feel at home, I don't get it.

Shaking her head again with this amazing look on her face, Grandma Mattie said he wanted to do married things. Oh she said I see now what you are talking about said Sister Pauline.

"Like I said, I'm still praying for you and Jessie." Grandma Mattie said.

Sister Viola then spoke up and said so I asked him to leave and not to come back anymore. I really thought that he was the one too. He goes to church and he is the head deacon of his church.

Grandma Mattie turned and looked at her and gave her a smile and said and why do you think that he is any different from any other man. He's a man isn't he? Now what you should have done is talked to him first and let him know that you don't operate like that. Then if he didn't want to reason with you; then you should have showed him the door. Well I didn't Sister Viola said.

I tell you what I'm going to do she said. I'm going to see If Mr. Washington has a gentleman friend that might be interested in going out with us on a date; and I will tell him about you so that I can bring you along on the date with us. You mean that you would do that for me Sister Viola said.

Grandma Mattie said yes I would I would rather do this for you; than to see you out here looking for a man. You see I don't know how to tell you this Viola, but you aren't as young as we used to be. So when you reach our age, we have to have the hook up connection. You know what I mean. I see what you mean Sister Viola said.

Why you see what happen to me; well I didn't go looking for anyone; no not anyone; why he came to me thru my granddaughter and that's just exactly what you are going to have to do; is let this man come looking for you.

Sister Viola was beginning to see where Grandma Mattie was coming from, so she turned to her and said ok, I will be looking forward to this day.

Grandma Mattie was feeling good about herself right now, because she was thinking of how she was able to help one of her sister out in her church; you could really tell that she was a godly women and loved to help people. Then she said; you know we sister have got to look out for each other now. Sister Hattie Mae replied and said, yes we most certainly do.

Then they all started getting up and getting ready to leave and say their goodbye to each other when Sister Ida Mae says, I can't wait to meet this Mr. Berry Washington Sister Mattie. Grandma Mattie replied and said Um I bet you can't. Then they all walked out of the restaurant together.

3

MR. WASHINGTON TAKE GRANDMA MATTIE TO THE PARK

It's time for Mr. Washington to take Grandma Mattie for a stroll through the park on this bright sunny Saturday afternoon. And you can rest a sure that Mr. Washington knows how to take charge and make this day a day that she can remember.

"Mrs. Mattie would you like to sit here? Mr. Washington said."

Looking over at the bench while they were approaching it she said why sure; then after she had taken her seat she said; this is a really a nice park and this was a good day for us to come too. Mr. Washington cleared his throat and spoke up with his deep voice and said; yes it was a good day for us to come here.

"The two of them were silent for a few minutes looking at each other and smiling; when the both of them tried to speak at the same time." They both said I want to; Grandma Mattie smiled and said, oh I'm sorry, go ahead. Then Mr. Washington being the kind man that he was said no ladies first Ms. Mattie.

She then laughed and turned to him and said; ok, I was just going to say thank you again for asking me to spend the day with you; this was really a surprise to me; but I can truly say that it was a good surprise.

Mr. Washington turned and looked into Grandma Mattie eyes and said you are quite Welcomed Ms. Mattie; and you might not believe what I'm going to say; but I'm glad that you decided to come with me today and I really like going places with you. Tell me are there some other places that you might have in mind that you would like to go to or something's that you would like to do?

Grandma Mattie started thinking of some places and things that she would like to do; now that she has been given a chance to do them. She wanted to make sure that she could name some of those places. So she spoke up and said; well let me see, I heard that they have a really good play coming up soon.

Really; what's the name of it Mr. Washington said? Grandma Mattie replied and said, I think they said; Chantel Leaves the Nest. He then said that sounds like it would be a good one to watch. Well, the commercial that they showed looked like it would be Grandma Mattie said.

Mr. Washington raised his back up off the bench and looked at Ms. Mattie with a smile and said; ok then, I would love to take you; just let me know when you want to go. She replied and said oh I would really like that and I think that it's nice of you to want to take me.

It's not a problem at all, like I said just let me know when you would like to go some places and I will be more than glad to take you he said.

In the midst of their laughing and talking to one another; a couple starts to walk by; Grandma Mattie looks at him and then looks toward the couple; when she looks back at him he is still looking at her. This made Grandma Mattie feel good because the lady that was walking by had on some short shorts; and he never took his eyes off her. This reaction caught her attention and she was please with him giving her all of his attention.

Grandma Mattie started thinking of how he was always trying to please her. She had never heard him mention anything that he liked to do; so she then said to him ok, but I'm always hearing you ask me what are some of the things that I like to do, but I never hear you say anything about some of the things that you like to do.

Mr. Washington turned and looked at her and said, well to be honest with you Ms. Mattie; as long as I'm with you this is all that matters. You see we have a lot in common; I really like some of the very same things that you do, but I just haven't been doing them until now; and why not Ms. Mattie said?

"Believe it or not I just hadn't met that special lady yet; to do these things with and now that I've meant you. I've enjoyed every minute of your time." Mr. Washington said.

When he said this to her; she started laugh and feeling like she really was special and then she said; oh stop that you are just saying that. Mr. Washington replied and said, no I'm not Ms. Mattie you see when you meet that special one you know when it is right for you; and I really feel like you are that special one.

Grandma Mattie started to think of how nice Mr. Washington was being to her and she could feel by the way that he was talking to her that he had been as lonely as she once was. She then said I don't really know what to say.

He then turned and looked at her again and said all I'm going to say is just keep on telling me the things that you like doing and I'm going to do everything that I can to make it happen. You are so nice to me she replied and he said; that's what a man is suppose to do.

Grandma Mattie turns and looks at Mr. Washington and gives him a smile then she looks across the park at the water and says; oh doesn't that water look nice over there; why it reminds me of when I used to go to the beach. So you like going to the beach you say. Mr. Washington said.

At this very moment her mind had started too wondered back to when she was young and she would go to the beach from time to time. She then said yes I do, why I used to go a lot when I was younger; and my husband used to take me occasionally every once and a while too; but it has been a long time since I've been to one.

Would you like to go again sometimes? Mr. Washington said.

Grandma Mattie replied and said oh I would love to go. Ok, I will see what I can do about that he said. She had begun to realize more and more that she was in the company of a powerful spirit from the way that he was acting and sounding. Hope that I'm not saying too much am I? She surprisingly said, why not at all he said.

Now Grandma Mattie was pleased to know that this wasn't one of those men's that you got out of a cracker jack box; instead he was summing up to be more of a leader; one that could be an example for a lot of the men's around here today.

Then suddenly Grandma Mattie just remembered that she needed to ask Mr. Washington something. So she turned and looked at him and said; can I ask you something if you don't mind me asking? Why sure go ahead and ask me he said.

Well I have a dear friend that I wanted to see if you had a real nice gentleman friend that would love to go out to eat with us sometimes. She's really a nice lady and she's been a widow for seven years now.

Mr. Washington replied back and said that wouldn't be a problem Ms. Mattie; I will be meeting with the men from the church in a few weeks; so I can ask one of them then. Oh would you Grandma Mattie said.

Yes I can. And we can set it up for a Saturday or on a day that's convenient for the both of you. You see, I have some engagement coming up on the next couple of Saturday's, he said. Ms. Mattie agreed and said that will be alright with me and I will tell Sister Viola; I know that she is going to be looking forward to going out with us. Very well then Ms. Mattie he replied.

Mr. Washington was wondering if Ms. Mattie was beginning to want something to eat; so he said would you like to get something to eat Ms. Mattie. Yes I believe that I would she replied; but if I had known that we were coming here to the park today. I would have fixed a basket dinner for us.

Not this time, but I will take a rain check on it he said; that's a deal and I'm going to have Bennie fix your favorite, a big slab of those barbeque ribs. Grandma Mattie said. Now that would be right on time he said.

They started getting up to leave and while they were talking and walking to the car; Grandma Mattie said; this was really nice. Mr. Washing replied and said I'm glad that you liked it Ms. Mattie.

4

UNCLE JESSIE CALLS SISTER PAULINE

Uncle Jessie is sitting there at the table eating his breakfast all alone thinking about his wife Sister Pauline. He looked across the table at the empty chair that she used to sit in when they would have breakfast together. He did this very same thing practically every morning and he kept a picture frame of them sitting on the table as well. He would just sit there for hours looking at her picture.

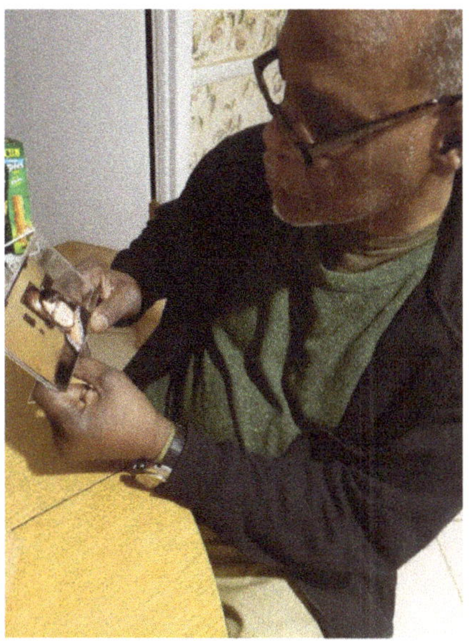

Things just weren't the same anymore since she wasn't there to have breakfast and to talk to him like they used to do. Why it was just like the Kings and Queen in the palace the way that he would set things up for her every day.

He really missed her and he wanted her to come home too; but he knew that he had to make some changes before that would happen. The changes that he hadn't been ready to do in order for her to come back home yet.

You see Uncle Jessie never wanted to go to church unless there was a funeral and this would upset Sister Pauline so bad. She would ask him to go almost every Sunday morning; he would always give her the excuse that he didn't have anything to wear or that he wasn't ready yet.

She being the kind and gentle person that she was, she would never argue with him; she would just go right on into the room and start getting ready and go on to church by herself without him.

Uncle Jessie liked staying at home because he liked taking his sips every now and then from his happy juice bottle that he hides. He thought that Sister Pauline didn't know about it; but she came across it while she was cleaning up one day and she could smell it on his breath when she would come home from church on every Sunday afternoon. So she just covered it back up and kept right on cleaning.

Sister Pauline never mentioned this to Uncle Jessie because she knew that it would start an argument and make things worse between them. So she would go on just like there wasn't anything going on just to keep peace between them.

She loved Uncle Jessie very dearly and you could always tell the difference in him though when he had had a sip of that old happy juice; why she would make sure that he had clean clothes, she cooked his meals and she would always make sure that he was taken care of. He was the same way with her too. He would work and bring a portion of his money home and give her and make sure that the bills were paid. Then he would always manage to save a little extra out for his happy juice. That's what a good man does for his lady and his home.

When Uncle Jessie first meant Sister Pauline he was at the grocery store picking him up some grocery for that week. Right, when he had turned to go over on the other aisle is when he laid his eyes on her and he thought that he had seen the prettiest lady in the world. She was something to look at; she had a short cut hair style with a very pretty smile and she looked good from her head to her feet. Why he couldn't hardly take his eyes off her.

She had noticed him looking at her so she smiled back and kept on putting some grocery in her cart.

He walked pass her and smiled and spoke, then as he was walking pass her he looked back and just shook his head. So he proceeded to finish shopping and headed for the check-out counter.

When he looked she was on her way there at the same time. So he asked her to go ahead of him. While they were standing there waiting in line; he cleared his throat and introduced himself to her and she did the same back to him. He then started a conversation with her and asked her for her phone number.

Uncle Jessie thought that now would be a good time as any, he felt like if he didn't do this and let her leave without getting it he might not ever see her again. Then she gave it to him and smiled and proceeded to place her grocery onto the counter top. Aw you should have seen Uncle Jessie then he was grinning from ear to ear like a chest cat they used to say.

Why he couldn't wait to get home and put the grocery up so that he could call her so that they could get better acquainted and that's how they met. Once he called her then he asked her over for dinner he loved to cook, so he cooked a meal for them.

While Uncle Jessie was sitting there going back down member lane; he thought that he would call Sister Pauline and see how she was doing.

This wasn't the first time that he had called her. Why he would call her practically every day just to see how she was doing.
As soon as he was done eating; he then went into the living room and sat down in his rocking chair and made the call to her. She

picked up the phone and said good morning Jessie; she had caller Id, so she could tell who was calling her.

He replied back and said good morning Pauline; how are you doing this morning? She said I'm doing just fine and what about you. He said I'm alright.

Then she said what do you want Jessie; I didn't really want anything I was just checking to see how you were doing. I see she said.

Aunt Pauline wouldn't admit it but she was missing Uncle Jessie just as much as he was missing her. She tries to stay busy most of the time. She really enjoyed when he would call her to talk to her. I would imagine that if he didn't call her on a daily basis she would be really lonely.

All of a sudden Uncle Jessie had a thought that made him realize that he needed to go back to doing the things that he used to do so that this would make the both of them happy once again. So he spoke up and said Pauline how would you like to come over for dinner? Her response was what do you have going on Jessie? He laughed and said why does there have to have to be something going on. I just felt like cooking a meal and I wanted to know if you would like coming over and eat with me.

Now, Uncle Jessie could cook that's one of the trades that he learned from Grandma Mattie. She taught all her girls and the boys how to cook clean and how to take care of things.

This was one of the things that Pauline liked about Jessie; he could burn some food now. She started thinking about when they first laid eyes up on each other. She will never forget the first time that he had her over to his house for dinner. He had Beef Roast, carrots, potatoes, cornbread, green beans, and he could make the best sweet tea. Not to mention he could make the best chest pie.

Why just thinking about it made her mouth water for it. He was always so attentive of her to make sure she had everything she needed and that she was comfortable. That's the Jessie that she once knew and loved.

It's just that over the years he had changed a little; he wasn't mean to her and he could still cook; but for some strange reason he just let the happy juice come between them and they were not doing the things that they used to do together anymore.

Since there has been some time past between them Uncle Jessie had finally realized what happen to them and he was ready to start making some changes she thought. So she paused and then said, well I guess I can Jessie.

You couldn't see him over the phone but he was smiling and he was so happy that she had accepted his invitation to come over for dinner that evening. She asked if he would like for her to bring anything when she came. He said no all I need for you to do is come ready to eat. She then laughed and said alright then Jessie.

They talked for a little while longer and then they got off the phone. Pauline starting thinking about Jessie more and more now that she was going to be meeting up with him in a few days. So she decided that she needed to send up a special prayer for them.

And little that she knew that across town Uncle Jessie was praying too; and if Pauline had known this, why she would have been shouting and jumping for joy.

All she ever wanted was to see Uncle Jessie sitting beside her in church every Sunday.

5

MR. WASHINGTON IS HAVING LUNCH WITH THE MEN ON SATURDAY

The men are all sitting at the table eating and talking to one another; when Mr. Washington speaks up and says tell me how has things been going Deacon Richard? Deacon Richard was a tall slender man that wore glasses and he had a mustache.

Deacon Richard replied and said; things have been going good; why, I brought me a new truck the other day. Is that right? Mr. Washington said. Deacon Richard was a man that spoke with authority when he would speak.

He went on to explain and said; yes that's right. Why, the transmission went out on my old one. I had that truck for about eighteen years now.

Mr. Washington knew that Deacon Richard was a man that liked to hold on to things for a very long time and he's money too. He had money but he was tight with it; he would give a charitable donation to the church every once and a while though.

Well I guess with having it that long, it was time for another one. Mr. Washington said. Deacon Richard replied and said yes it was it went the last mile that it could go, anyway how have you been doing?

I've been doing good, just trying to keep busy. Mr. Washington replied.

Deacon Bill stopped eating long enough to say I know what you mean. I've been busy planting some tomato seeds and green beans. I thought that I would start me another late garden this year.

Deacon Bill was an old farmer who lived along; he was always raising his crops and giving most of it away. That was the kind of person that he was; he was a kind and gentle man with a lot of love in his heart.

Well I'll start making room in my freezer for my part. Mr. Washington said. Alright said Deacon Bill and I should have some turnip greens to give you to pretty soon. Mr. Washington laughed and said; now you know that I love me some turnip greens don't you. Yes I do and I haven't forgotten you either. Deacon Bill said. Good I will be looking for them. Mr. Washington said. Ok replied Deacon Bill.

Evening Deacon Beasley is everything going alright with you? Mr. Washington said.

Deacon Beasley was another one of the deacons that came out to eat with them; he was a medium frame man with short hair; he liked to talk a lot and he was married to Corrine.

Well I'm doing as well as to be expected he said. You know I had to go to the doctor the other day about my knee it's been giving me trouble every now and then. Is that right; well we are going to have prayer for you before we leave this evening if that would be alright with you. Mr. Washington said. That will be just fine. Deacon Beasley said. Mr. Washington could tell by looking at Deacon Beasley that he was really worried about his knee; so he said consider it done. Thank you; Deacon Beasley said; he replied you are welcomed.

"Oh and could you say a prayer for my wife too while you are at it. It's getting closer to time for her to have her surgery." Deacon Beasley said.

Mr. Washington had almost forgotten about Sister Corrine surgery; so then he said that's right; when is the date again that she will be having her surgery? It will be next Monday Deacon Beasley said. Alright then we will say a prayer for her too. Mr. Washington said.

Deacon Beasley said I show do appreciate you doing this for her and me. Well it's not a problem I would do it for you and anybody else that needs prayer, that's what I'm here for.

I sure do wish that you would say one for me and my family too. We are having a hard time this year with me being laid off from work now for three months. Deacon Beasley said.

Mr. Washington spoke up and said I had been meaning to ask you had they called you back to work yet. No they haven't and I've been looking for something to help me out on the side he said. I've just started getting my unemployment but it's not enough to pay all my bills.

Deacon Beasley raised his back from his chair turned and looked at him and said, well I can't pay that much; but I sure could use some help getting my hay put up if you are interested.

"I would be glad to help you; and it would help me put some food on my table too." Deacon Bill said.

Deacon Beasley replied and said; alright then you can start on Monday if that's alright with you. That would be just fine with me; Deacon Bill said and I want to thank you for considering me for the job. "Why it was my pleasure." Deacon Beasley said.

Brother Bob had just arrived he was running late; due to he was a barber and he was still cutting his last customer hair. He greeted everyone and apologized for being late to the luncheon.

They really have some good food here don't they. Deacon Richard said.

Deacon Beasley spoke up and said; yes they do. That's why I like coming here to give my wife a break every now and then. I also like it when we meet here once a month. There's nothing wrong with that. Deacon Richard said.

Deacon Beasley started thinking about his wife Corrine; they had been together for over thirty five years now; so he looked at Deacon

Richard and said; you know I don't know what I would do if something happen to Corrine.

I'm sure she is going to do fine. Deacon Richard said. I sure hope so said Deacon Beasley; why she does all the cooking for me and cleaning up the house. Why we made a deal when we got married.

What deal was that Deacon Beasley? Deacon Richard said. That she would take care of the inside of the house and that I would take care of the outside; and we have been doing this for 35 years. Deacon Beasley said. Is that right? Deacon Richard said.

Yes it is, so now you can see that I would be lost without her said Deacon Beasley.

Deacon Richard could hear a little sadness in Deacon Beasley voice; so he wanted to reassure him that everything was going to be alright. So he looked over at him and said; yes I do, but now don't you go getting yourself all worked up. She is going to come thru this surgery with flying colors and she's going to be up cooking them good meals once again.

That's right Deacon Beasley; just keep the faith and everything is going to be alright. Mr. Washington said. Deacon Beasley replied and said; I sure will.

Mr. Washington just remembered that old habit that Deacon Beasley had; so he spoke up and said; now Deacon Beasley, I don't want to hear of you going down to the Juju Joint while Sister Corrine is in the hospital. Mr. Washington said.

Deacon Beasley looked around and answered him so fast you would have thought he was running a race. Why ever since I had that last attack and it took me a week to get over it; I haven't been back since.

You see I made a promise to keep an eye on Deacon Beasley while Sister Corrine was in the hospital. Deacon Bill said.

That's good; there is nothing like Brothers looking out for each other in times like these; well let's all join hands so that we can have a word of prayer now. Mr. Washington said.

Everyone joins hands so that they can have prayer; and Mr.

Washington leads them in prayer. Then he turns and looks at Deacon Beasley and says; well Deacon Beasley, I know that God's going to take care of Sister Corrine; and I want you to know that we are going to be keeping on praying for the both of you. Mr. Washington said. Deacon Beasley replied and said; why thank you and I really do appreciate you praying for us.

No problem, now you take care of yourself ok and if you need anything. I'm just a phone call away. Mr. Washington said. Deacon Beasley replied and said ok.

Brother Bob spoke up and told the men that even though he was late he still enjoyed the fellowship with them. They all agreed that they had a good time fellowshipping with one another.

Everybody was shaking hands and saying their good bye; when Mr. Washington spoke out to everyone and said; It was really good to see all of you again and the Lords will we will meet her again next month. And they all agreed.

"Oh Deacon Richard may I have a word with you?" Mr. Washington said. Why sure he replied. I was wondering what you were doing on next Saturday? I wanted to see if you would like to go out to dinner with me and a couple of sisters from the church.

Deacon Richard took a few minutes to think to make sure he didn't have anything planned. Then he said I can't say that I'm doing much of anything right now.

Good then I will pick you up around 3:00 p.m. if that's alright with you said Mr. Washington. Deacon Richard replied and said; alright I will see you then.

6

MR. WASHINGTON GOES TO MEET GRANDMA MATTIE

Grandma Mattie is at home sitting in her rocking chair reading her Bible and enjoying the evening when all of a sudden she hears the door bell ring. She gets up from her rocking chair and goes to the window and looks outside; then she sees Mr. Washington standing on the front porch. So she starts fixing her hair to make sure she looks good and pressing her hands over her dress to make sure it was straight. Then she goes to the door and says who is it? Mr. Washington spoke up and said it's Mr. Washington. Then she starts fixing her hair again and then she opened the door and asked him to come in.

Mr. Washington entered into the door smiling at Ms. Mattie and said why hello Mrs. Mattie, how are you doing today.

She was standing there with a great big smile on her face and replied back and said; well I'm doing just fine; I was just sitting here reading my Bible and then I was going to watch Gun Smoke my favorite show, you know I like seeing Festus.

As they were walking over toward the couch and her rocking chair to take their seats. He remembered her telling him how much she loved that show.

Mr. Washington then said; yes ma'am I do remember you telling me how much you love that show. Grandma Mattie looked at Mr. Washington and said yes I really do; now tell me what brings you over here today.

Mr. Washington cleared his throat and looked over at Ms. Mattie and said; well I've got some good news to share with you. You had asked me if I knew of a man friend for Sis. Viola so we could all go out to dinner sometimes. Grandma Mattie said yes I did, did you find someone she asked him?

Mr. Washington smiled and said well as a matter of fact I did, I spoke with one of the Deacons from the church and he is really looking forward to meeting Sis Viola.

Grandma Mattie stopped rocking and turned and looked at Mr. Washington and said you did, well that sounds good. So I will call her a little later and tell her the good news I'm sure that she's going to be just as happy as the Deacon is. Mr. Washington said I sure hope so.

Grandma Mattie just couldn't believe the good news that Mr. Washington had shared with her. Sis Viola was going to be going on a date and she wouldn't have to be out here looking for a man. Ms. Mattie spoke up and said; I want to thank you for doing that for me. It was my pleasure. Mr. Washington said.

Grandma Mattie started thinking if this would be a good time or not to ask Mr. Washington some question about this Deacon that he had asked to go out with them. So she paused for a minute and then looked over at him and said; do you mind if I ask you something? Mr. Washington replied and said why not at all go ahead and ask me.

Grandma Mattie laughed and said; I don't mean to sound nosey or anything, but could you tell me a little bit of something about him, so that I can kind fill Sister Viola in own a few things.

Mr. Washington smiled and said why not at all. Let's see where I can start, well he is a deacon of the church where I go. He's a clean cut, dresses real sharp, 6'2", well manner gentleman and he just brought him a new truck.

She had to raise straight up out of her rocking chair to the edge and took two quick looks at Mr. Washington and said, is that right, well I think that she is going to like this Deacon. He sounds like he has all the right things. Mr. Washington speaks up and says; excuse me.

Grandma Mattie realized that she might have spoken just a little too hasty; so she then said what I was meaning to say was that he sounds like he cares his self like a man that knows how to treat a lady.

Mr. Washington said yes he does; and I failed to mention that he is the head Deacon of the church. Grandma Mattie said he is. He replied and said yes he is. Oh ok she said; does he have any children? Has he ever been married before or have a job?

Hold on now slow your horses Mr. Washington said; he then looked over at her and said well let me see as a matter of fact he does have 3 children, he has been married before, but she died several years ago and he owns a farm out near the Blueberry Lake area. Grandma Mattie looked around batted her eyes a few times and said; why you don't mean.

Mr. Washington replied back and said yes I do mean, why he has blessed the church with a lot of gifts since he has been there.

Grandma Mattie clapped her hands together and started rocking back and forth and then she said; yes, Lord, Yes Lord, I think that she's done hit a gold mine. Mr. Washington really couldn't make out what all he had heard Ms. Mattie say; so he said; I'm sorry I didn't hear you.

Grandma Mattie calmed down and said; oh I was just saying that he seems to be a very nice man that's all. Yeah he's going to be a real nice man for her she mumbled under her voice. I'm glad that you feel that away Mrs. Mattie, because I would hate to disappoint you or Sis Viola. Mr. Washington said.

Grandma Mattie mind was going about 90 miles per minute now that she had heard what all Mr. Washington had said about Deacon Richard; she then said no she's not going to be disappointed in fact she is going to be very happy. I'm so glad that you feel that way he said.

I hope that you didn't mind me asking about him; you see Mrs. Mattie has to check things out to make sure that he's going to be right for her. Yes I most definitely understand and I'm glad that you asked about him. Believe me I do understand and I was telling him about her, from the conversation that you and I had about her; I really think that they are going to hit it off real good.

Well only time will tell. Yes surrey only time will tell. Ms. Mattie said.

Mr. Washington was beginning to get a little tired from the long day that he had. So he then looked over at Ms. Mattie and said well I guess that I had better get going. Oh but before I go, do you know what day that would be best for us to sit this date up for them.

Well let me see. I think that around the 1st of next month will be good. Because I'm going to be busy the next 2 weeks. I'm still taking my dance classes and I've added some swimming lessons on Saturday's, so that I can get ready for when we go to the beach. Ms. Mattie said.

Mr. Washington was tickled to see that Ms. Mattie was taking swimming class as well as dancing classes. He was starting to think that if he doesn't catch up with her, she is going to go off and leave him behind. He then said that is nice.

Grandma Mattie replied and said oh you are just saying that to be nice to me. No I'm really glad to see you working toward going on that trip that we had spoke about, now I need to get me some classes scheduled so that I will be ready. He said. Why thank you, well you go ahead and do that and you can call me a little later that would be fine with me.

Alright then I will do that so I will talk to later Mr. Washington said. He gets up and walks over to the door and says his goodbye. Grandma Mattie says ok, thanks for dropping by and thank you again for setting Sis Viola up on this date. Mr. Washington said it was no problem I enjoyed doing it. Well bye!!!

Ms. Mattie couldn't wait for Mr. Washington to leave so that she could call Sister Viola and tell her the good news. She then walks over to the couch and takes a seat; then she proceeds to call Sis Viola. Hello, Sis Viola, Yes this is Sis Viola,

Yes this is Sis Mattie, and I just called to tell you that my friend Mr. Washington came over to see me today and he just left. He came bearing some good news. And what news was that Sis Viola said. He told me that he had found you a man said, Ms. Mattie. He did, said, sister Viola. Yes he did, and I really think that you are going to like him too from what all he has told me about him.

Sister Viola had started smiling from ear to ear then she said is that right. Yes that's right. Let me fill you in on some of the things that he told me about him. Sis Viola replied and said ok,

Grandma Mattie started thinking of the things that Mr. Washington had told her about Deacon Richard. So she then said well let me see, he said that he was a sharp dresser, clean cut, 6'2" tall, he has 3 children, he has been married before but she's gone on home to glory, god rest her soul and he just brought a new truck, and take a wild guess where he lives

Sis Viola said, women I don't know. Why he lives out near Blueberry Lake, Ms. Mattie said. Sis Viola says sounds like he's got a little money living out there.

Ms. Mattie speaks up and says yes it does, so I set your date up for the 1ˢᵗ of the month. I was trying to wait until you got your check you know so that you could buy you something new. That was awfully sweet of you Sis Mattie and I want to thank you, she said.

Grandma Mattie said you are welcomed!!! So you can stop looking now and get ready for this big day. Alright then said Sister Viola: I can't hardly wait till the 1ˢᵗ of the month, well I've already got butter flies jumping around in my stomach.

Now don't go getting yourself all worked up now; Ms. Mattie said. Everything is going to be just fine. Ok Sister Viola said I will talk to you later. Ok Bye now said Grandma Mattie.

Sister Viola had some thoughts of her own when she got off the phone; she was thinking of how she might be equal with this man. You see Sister Viola husband had left her well off and she lived in a real nice neighborhood. She has 4 bedrooms, 2 baths and a 2 car garage brick home. Not to mention her bank account was pretty fat too.

So from the way that Mr. Washington described Deacon Richard he seemed like he was going to be just the right match for Sister Viola.

7

IT'S THE FIRST OF THE MONTH AND IT'S TIME FOR THE DATE

A couple of weeks have passed by and the ladies have been talking on the phone before their dates arrive to take them out. They all get into the car and head over to the restaurant. On the way there everyone seemed to be quiet. Ms. Mattie could sense something strange going on but she didn't say anything. Mr. Washington was beginning to notice too, but he just kept on driving to the restaurant.

Then they arrived parked the car opened the doors for the ladies and then went inside were they were seated. It was still quiet until Sister. Mattie spoke up and said, Sister Viola you really look nice this evening. Why, thank you Sister Mattie, why you do too Sister Viola said. Thank you said, Sister. Mattie.

Mr. Washington could see that Deacon Richard was lost for words; so he said Deacon Richard do you have anything that you would like to say?

Deacon Richard runs his hand across his face and say, I just wanted to thank you for asking me to come out with you all this evening. And Ms. Viola, you do look very nice this evening. And so do you Mrs. Mattie.

Both of the Ladies say. Thank You. Then everyone starts looking at their menu; everyone was still silent while they were looking; then within a few minutes Mr. Washington asked them if they are ready to order.

Sister Viola was thinking I can't seat here another minute without talking to Sister Mattie. So she spoke up and said, well I would like to be excused to the ladies room before I do that, that is if you don't mind. Why not at all Mr. Washington said.

She then looked over at Sis Mattie and said would you like to accompany me please? Sister Mattie looked over at Sister Viola and said, why sure I will, Mr. Washington and Deacon Richard, will you excuse us while we go to the ladies room we will be right back.

Mr. Washington and Deacon Richard said alright ladies, then they stood up out of courtesy and helped the ladies with their chair and then they sat back down.

As they got up and started toward the ladies room, the men begin to start talking about the ride over to the restaurant. Mr. Washington was shaking his head and then he looked over toward Deacon Richard and said; what's wrong Deacon Richard you have been quiet every since we pick up Sis Viola.

Deacon Richard looked down at the table and took a deep breath and said; shaking his head; well I wasn't going to say anything. Mr. Washington had this surprising look on his face and said well speak up Deacon Richard and let me know what's going on.

Ok, well I just wanted to say that I already know Sis Viola and when you told me about this date, I didn't know that she was going to be the one that I would be meeting and he dropped his head again. Poor man looked like he was about to cry.

Mr. Washington already knew that something wasn't right when he wasn't talking on the way over here. Then he said, is that so. Deacon Richard replied and said yes, and stared shaking his head again and said; now I really feel bad. Cause I don't know what to say to her.

Mr. Washington lean back in his seat and looked over to Deacon Richard and said; let me ask you something, did you try one of those player moves on her? Yes I did he said.

So that explains why this is not starting off as well, let me ask something else. Do you still like her? Deacon Richard looked over at Mr. Washington and said, yes as a matter of fact I do I just stuck my foot in my mouth when I was over her house one day and every since then I really regret what I said.

Mr. Washington was still looking at Deacon Richard and he said, well now would be a good time for you to apologize and set the record straight with Sister Viola. You see we all are human and sometimes we let the flesh take over and it gets the best of us; when we should be praying for God to give us strength to endure the situation and to overcome our desire.

You are right and that's just what I'm going to do he said. Good Mr. Washington said, now that's how a real man handles his business.

Meanwhile, the ladies were still in the ladies room talking about why Sister Viola was so quiet on the way over here to the restaurant. Grandma Mattie was looking into the mirror while she was putting some more lipstick on her lips and then she said, woman what is wrong with you, you have been quiet every since we picked you up from the house.

Sister Viola took a deep breath and leaned back against the wall and said; well I don't know how to tell you this Sis Mattie. Grandma Mattie could see that she had something serious to tell her; so she said tell me what? Go on and just say it that's the only way you are going to be able to tell me.

Well here it goes, Remember when I was telling you that I had meant a man a while back. She replied and said, yes I remember. Sis Viola took another deep breath and said, and you remember me telling you that he was wonting to collect and that he was the head Deacon of the church.

Yes she said, then after thinking about what Sister Viola had just said, she was stung and quickly said, are you trying to tell me what I think you are trying to tell me.

Sis Viola said, yes that's right. It's him it was Deacon Richard; why I didn't think that I would ever see him again.

Sister Mattie gave her another look; but this look was a look of compassion; and then she said well I can understand; and I don't blame you for feeling the way that you do; but let me ask you something; how do you still feel about him now? Now be honest with me.

Sis Viola was hesitating in answering Sister Mattie; and then she came back with saying; well I feel like maybe I might have made a mistake in sending him away that night.

Sister Matter looked into her face and she could see that she still had some feelings for this man. So she grabbed her hand and said, sometimes we have to pay a little price to have a little happiness in swallowing our pride; so are you ready to put your big granny panties on and let's set the record straight.

Sis Viola smiled and said I can try; good then; Sister Mattie got your back on this one. Just take your time and talk to him and let him know that you didn't appreciate what happen and that you are willing to put this all behind you and see where this can go from here.

Alright then she said, wish me luck,

Sister Mattie started laughing and said, you are going to do just fine just because you weren't ready then to sit him straight; doesn't mean that you shouldn't have to give up on someone that might want to be in your future someday. You know what I mean.

Sis Viola spoke up and said I see what you mean Sis Mattie.

Alright then are you ready to go back out here and make the best of this night; after all we don't have to pay for our dinner; they are going to be paying and we should enjoy ourselves. Why sure I am she replied.

They walk back out to the table and took their seat. Sister Viola and Deacon Richard started looking at each and they both speak up and the same time and say; I'm sorry, then they started laughing at each other like High school kids.

Mr. Washington then looks over to Ms. Mattie and nodes his head and Ms Mattie smiled and nodded her head as well. That was a sign that everything was going to be alright with these two. They hated to know that they had done all this hard work in putting these two together and then it wouldn't work out for them.

Will you forgive me Sister Viola for my unkindly behavior he said, Sister Viola looked over at Deacon Richard and said, yes I will we should have talked about this before I asked you to leave that night.

Yes we should have but Its' not your fault, I was out of line and I don't blame you for asking me to leave, but I will promise you this one thing; that it will never happen again and thank you for accepting my apology. I hope that this want be our last time going out.

Sis Viola smiled at him and said, I would love to go out again with you and I think that we were given another chance for a reason.

Yes I believe we were too, and now that we have cleared this up this matter; I would like to invite you to our pastor Anniversary in October, if you don't have anything going on then.

Oh I would really like that she said. It's a date then he said with a sign of relief. He had been sitting on pins and needles that night up until they were able to clear this matter up. Now everything was going good with them.

Mr. Washington was proud of Deacon Richard in how he handled his situation with Sister Viola. He could see that by him speaking to him about the right thing for him to do; was the best advice that he could have given him. He could also see that these two were really liking each other.

Besides, Mr. Washington hadn't always been in the position that he was in now. So he could relate to Deacon Richard and try to give him some advice and to help keep him on this narrow path that he was on. Remember now what he had said at their monthly meeting; brothers should look out for each other and show love toward one another; especially when you see them in the wrong and headed for destruction.

Well are you all ready to order now Mr. Washington said. I believe that we are said Deacon Richards. What would you like to order Mrs. Viola? She takes another look at menu again and says let me see.

8

IT'S THE NEXT DAY AND SISTER VIOLA CALLS SISTER MATTIE

Sister Viola is at home laying out on the bed her dress, earrings, necklace, bracelet, stocking, under garments and her wide brim hat. She is preparing to go to church today. When suddenly she thought of calling Sister Mattie to thank her again for the big night that she had last night.

So she walks into her living room and sat down in her recliner and makes the call to Sister Mattie. Then when she hears Sister Mattie picked up on the other end; she says hello Sister Mattie how are doing this morning? Sister Mattie replied and said I'm doing very well thank you and how are you doing? I'm blessed she said with excitement in her voice.

Sister Viola started out by saying I just wanted to call you and thank you again for making last night special for me. Why it has been a long time since I have felt as good as I did last night and I really do appreciate it from the bottom of my heart.

Sister Mattie was smiling and replied back and said why I'm just glad that I could be of help to you. Like I had told you at our monthly meeting; we Sister's have got to stick together and look out for each other.

Yes you did, and I really do appreciate you looking out for me. I just wish that there were more Sister like you. Sister Mattie spoke up and said, now I'm not anything special; I just believe in giving help to someone when I see that they need it. Instead of sitting around putting someone down why not help them with their situation when you can.

"That is really sweet of you Sister Mattie and I will be keeping you in my prayers". Please do Sister Viola I just hope that I'm doing the right thing that's all. Just keep on praying and believing and God is going to work it out. You will see.

Oh and I wanted to tell you that Deacon Richard asked me to go with him to his pastor Anniversary in October. Yes I kind of heard him when he asked you last night. Not that I was ease dropping or trying to meddle, I just happen to overhear him while he was talking to you.

Yes he did and it made me feel so special and it should have made you feel special; because you are special and don't you ever forget that. I want she said.

You know I was thinking since him and Mr. Washington belong to the same church, this is going to make it easier for us to do a lot of things together. Sister Mattie said. You know I never thought of it like that; but now since you said that it does don't it.

Why Mr. Washington invited me and my family to the pastor Anniversary in October as well, well that was very nice of him Sister Viola said. Yes, it was and now that you are going that makes it even better.

See Sister Viola I told you that things were going to work out this time around with you and Deacon Richard. Yes you did and I'm glad that we were given another chance.

Sister Viola at this very moment realized that she had a true friend and she wanted to take the time and have a word of prayer with her. So she asked Sister Mattie if they could have a word of prayer together. Sister Mattie agreed and they had prayer while they were still on the phone.

Why thank you for having prayer with me Sister Mattie, and thank you for asking me Sister Viola.

Sister Viola, I'm going to share something with you and maybe I can help you understand why it was so important to me to see you happy too. Ok she said.

I didn't realize that I was as lonely as I was before my granddaughter introduced me to Mr. Washington. Now I feel like I was missing out on life living by myself and looking at these four walls. You know that good men are so hard to find, but by me waiting until now. I feel like God has given me what I needed and deserved. What do you mean by that Sister Mattie?

Well we don't always see what other people see in us; but if we all took the time to give a helping hand to one another we could all help that person or maybe even more people that needs our help.

Sister Mattie smiled and said and I couldn't be selfish in having my joy and not seeing my sister have joy too. You see that's what this journey is all about, and that's the way all of us should feel and try to look out more for one another and then we would have such a better world today.

Sister Viola spoke up and said; why after hearing you speak like that Sister Mattie; I feel like I've already been to church. You said that so well and I couldn't have said it any better. Then they laughed and chuckled together.

Aw I was just speaking the truth that's all. I've always been taught that if you can't say something nice about someone; don't say nothing at all, me too, me too.

You see God makes no mistakes; even when we don't understand a lot of things. God is always in the mix of it if we just let him. Sometimes we want to get ahead of him and he has to show us that he's in control and not we ourselves and the sooner that we learn that the better off that we will be.

You are most certainly right Sister Mattie. I want to thank you for sharing that with me; and Sister Mattie I want to leave this one thing with you; If I can ever do anything for you; please don't hesitate to ask me.

You don't owe me nothing you hear me, all I want you to do is to continue to pray for me and I will do the same for you; and that's all that we need to do for each other. I sure will she said, alright then, well I guess we had better get off this phone so that we can get ready for church. I think that you are right; so maybe we can talk a little later and I will see you at church; alright then, bye. Bye said Sister Mattie.

Sister Mattie looked over at her picture of her and the family and picked it up smiling; then she said; well Paw, pa I made Sister Viola happy yesterday and she want have to be alone now. Then she blew a kiss at the picture and sat the picture frame back down and went into the bedroom and started getting ready for church.

It's amazing if we could all take a little time out to do something for our sister and brothers to show them how much we love them and care for them. Not only would this help us, but it would help us teach this new generation called the millennium; how to be of good fruit too.

9

IT'S OCTOBER AND THEY ARE HAVING THR PASTOR ANNIVERSARY

A couple of months had gone by and the day has come for Mr. Washington and Deacon Richard pastor Anniversary. Mr. Washington stops by the takeout Ms. Mattie house to pick her up to take her to church with him.

He pulled up in a shiny red impala and it had the sharpest rims on it that you would ever want to see.

While they were walking to the car he noticed something a little different with Ms. Mattie; why she looked so good to him he asked her if he could take a picture of her. She turned and was smiling and said why sure you can and she posed for the picture.

Then he opened the door for her and then they proceed to travel to the church; he was driving just a little but slower than usual today; that was because he was enjoying the moment that he was spending with Ms. Mattie. He would look over at her from time to time on their way there and smile and she would also look his way and smile. They exchanged words every now and then and just kept on smiling.

Now Ms. Mattie has arrived at the church with Mr. Washington he gets out of the car and hands his camera to one of the members standing in front of the church. He asked her if she would mind taking a picture of him and Ms. Mattie. She took the camera and then said I would love to; so the picture was taken while he was helping her get out of the car; then after she took the picture, then they walk into the church.

He starts walking around introducing her to some of the members; then he made his way over too meet Deacon Beasley and his wife Sister Corrine he was a little fond of them.

This is Sis Corrine and Deacon Beasley he said, I would like for you all to meet Sis Mattie. They were standing there smiling and they looked so happy together. Ms. Mattie replied back and said, pleased to meet you all. They then said we are so glad that you could come to worship with us today. I'm glad that I could come too.

Then Mr. Washington ex courted Mrs. Mattie to her seat and then he said; Mrs. Mattie I'm going to let you sit here and I will get back with you after the service is over. Ms. Mattie said alright Mr. Washington. Oh but before I go may I get another picture of the both of us: she said why sure.

Grandma Mattie had on a white dress, sliver loop earrings, sliver necklace and a black mink fur coat with some black pumps and matching black purse.

She didn't ask him any questions about where he was going; she just thought that maybe he was one of the deacons of the church or maybe he was going to sit with the deacons to help them carry out the service. She then seen him walk over to one of the deacons and start talking about something that he was showing him in the book that they were looking at.

She then looked around and here comes Sister Viola and Deacon Richard coming through the doors. Sister Viola was smiling and so was Deacon Richard. This made Ms. Mattie so happy to see her friend coming thru the door smiling. He sat her down right beside Ms. Mattie then he said good morning Sister Mattie, glad to have you here with us today and they started hugging and shaking hands. Then she looked around again and some of her family was coming in.

This made her so happy she was smiling and greeting them as they were coming over to speak to her and giving her a hug.

She looked back around one more time at the door and she then seen the rest of her family coming in and shaking hands and speaking then they took their seats.

Then low and behold she seen her son Jessie and she couldn't believe that it was him. Why he was sharp and he looked like he hadn't been drinking either. He came and spoke to his mother and then he took his seat. This made Ms. Mattie so happy to see her son in church and not walking in with a bottle in his hand. Why he didn't even look like the same person he was so sharp.

Tina sat down right beside Grandma Mattie; and Grandma Mattie lean over and whispered in her ear and said, good job he really looks nice and I'm proud of you. Tina smiled back and said you can always count on me, Grandma Mattie.

She looked back around again at the door and she seen the rest of her family started coming in and shaking hands and speaking then they took their seats.

As she was waiting for the service to start someone poked her on her shoulder. When she looked around to see who it was, there sit Hattie Mae and Ida Mae smiling like to chest cats. She spoke to the both of them and turned around and continued to wait for the service to start.

Hattie Mae had on a black hat with feathers around it, and gray dress with a grey short cut jacket and she had a matching yellow and green looking necklace and earrings with black matching shoes, and purse so did Ida Mae have on similar colors as she did, she wore a black top with a black and white pin striped top with black shoes and her blouse had a rose on it.

When all the time she was thinking of how they have found out about it that we were coming to church here today. I declare I believe them women have psychic minds.

It was time to start the service now, so Deacon Richard stood up and announced that the service was beginning to start. He said we will now begin our services and turn the service over to our Mistress of Ceremony Sis. Corrine Beasley.

Sister Corrine stood up and said; before we begin our service for today, we will have the introduction of our proud Pastor by Deacon Richard after which we will have our Devotion.

Deacon Richard stood up and said good morning everyone we would like to welcome each and every one of you to our Pastor Anniversary, and we are so happy to be celebrating his Anniversary today; so I present to you our proud pastor, Rev. Berry Washington

Ms. Mattie eyes got as big as a half of dollar and she said "Oh Lord" and then she passes out. One of her grand children name Monique shouted out and said, Grandma Mattie has done passed out you'll.

Her family was concerned about her and they begun to start whispering and looking around. Tina was sitting by her and she started fanning her and asked for a glass of water for her to drink.

Mr. Washington speaks up and says you'll help Sis Mattie, you see sometimes things can be overwhelming, but there is a time and place for everything. We want to make sure that Sis Mattie is alright before we go ahead with our program for today.

One of the Ushers used some smelling sauce to help awake her; after she came too she looked around at the family and says he's a preacher man. Hallelujah***

Mr. Washington then smiled and said alright now we will turn our services back over into the hands of our Mistress of Ceremony Sis Corrine.

Sis Corrine stood up again and said now we will have our Deacons begin our Devotion services.

They then sung a song called "Jesus Is the Light".

There was prayer right after the song and then they followed with another song and then there was the reading of the scripture.

As the service continued the next song that was sung was "God is good", Grandma Mattie noticed the lady that was singing this song. Her name was Sister Harper; now this lady could really sing. She didn't realize that she was a member of this church. Sister Mattie had known her for quite some time now.

Sis Corrine then stood back up after the song and said thank you for the devotion and said it's good to see all of you here today to share this special occasion with us in celebrating our pastor Anniversary, again you are always welcomed here in the house of God. So please feel free to come back anytime. At this time we are going to have a Solo from Sis Pauline after which we will be taking up our collection.

Grandma Mattie had asked Sister Pauline to come because she felt bad that she didn't get to come to the cook-out; even though she and Jessie were separated; she was still a part of the family. So she had asked Mr. Washington if she could sing a solo on that day. He agreed and had her name added to the program. Sis Pauline stood up and sung her Solo. She was a singing sister; why she had such a beautiful voice. It would make you stand up and shout.

Shortly afterwards the Deacons arranged the service so that they could take up the offerings.

Then Sis Corrine said we want to thank Deacon Richard and the officers for taking up the offering and at this time we will be hearing from our proud Pastor Berry Washington.

Pastor Washington stood up and took this opportunity to introduce Ms. Mattie and to welcome her and her family and friends for coming to support him on this day. They didn't know that he was a pastor until today; he had wanted to surprise them on today.

Pastor Washington then preached the Sermon on Jesus is the

reason we made it and then he opened the doors of the church; asking if there was anyone that would like to choose god as their personal savior.

There was no one that came so then the service was turned back over to the Mistress of Ceremony Sister Corrine.

Sister Corrine took the floorer again and said; we want to thank Pastor Berry Washington for that great Sermon today and at this time we will be opening the floor for any remarks, afterwards we have some gifts that we would like to present to our pastor and then we will be hearing from our proud Pastor.

When Pastor Washington finished making his comments to the people for coming and the gifts that he received; Sis Corrine then said we want to thank each and every one of you for making this day possible for our pastor.

Sis Mattie was sitting there thinking that now would be a good time for her to stand up and make a remark on how she enjoyed the service. So she stood up and said I would like to make a remark. Sister Corrine said yes and took her seat and gave her the floor to speak.

Ms. Mattie says; well I just wanted to say thank you to Pastor Washington for asking me and my family to come to worship with you on this special day. I was really surprised on today, but I'm very glad that I could share this day with you all. Glad to know that this man is serving god and that he is a good and up standing pastor. We enjoyed ourselves and we will be coming back soon. Thank You!!!

Sis Corrine then said thank you Sister Mattie for those remarks and will there be any more Remarks or Announcements? If not then we will be have the closing Remarks from our Pastor Berry Washington.

Pastor Berry Washington stood up and gave his remarks and the benediction. Then they start shaking hands and saying their good Byes.

Ms. Mattie was still smiling and when Pastor Berry Washington approached her she said well I'm sorry if I disrupted the service today. He spoke up and said you are fine; I'm glad that you were able to be here on this day and that you have done found out that I am a pastor; I'm happy and satisfied.

ALL THE FAMILY MEETS OVER TO GRANDMA MATTIE HOUSE

The family had all gathered at Grandma Mattie house after church today. They were all laughing and shaking hands and hugging one another. Even Pauline and Jessie were holding hands and laughing on this day. Yeah that's right Pauline and Jessie came over after church too.

This was unusual but Grandma Mattie didn't think much of it; she just continued talking and looking around at how happy everybody was.

When suddenly one of the twin sisters spoke up and said I'm glad that Ida Mae and I decided to come to worship at Pine Valley Baptist Church today. Sister Hattie Mae said. Sis Mattie spoke up and said, I was wondering how did you all fine out that we were attending there today.

Sister Hattie Mae replied and said well sister Ida Mae and I haven't been there in a very long time and we decided to go this morning. Oh I see she said. When really Grandma Mattie was still thinking that they must had been listening thru that fence again.

They really had a nice service today and know that I think about it, that's where I have seen Pastor Washington at before. Grandma

Mattie said you have, so you had meant Pastor Washington before today. She replied and said yes it was a long time ago that we had gone there on a few different occasions.

Oh so you known Pastor Washington before today she said. Sister Hattie Mae replied and said not really, I just attended services there about a year ago and I told Tina that I thought I had seen him before somewhere.

Is that right Sister Mattie said, yes it is Sister Hattie Mae replied. Why once I see a face I never forget it. Plus he is a very nice looking man.

Sister Ida Mae decided she needed to break the ice between Sister Mattie and her sister. So she spoke and said to Sister Mattie. So you got you a preacher now for your man.

Sister Mattie turned and looked at Sister Ida Mae and said, yes I do, and I'm proud of it too.

Ida Mae just smiled and said well that's nice Sister Mattie. She said why thank you Sister Ida Mae.

Tina was standing close by when the conversation was going on between the twins and her Grandma Mattie. She could see that Grandma Mattie could take care of herself, but if she needed to, she was going to jump in on the conversation at any time.

Sister Hattie Mae felt like she needed to change the conversation to something else. So she spoke up and said why look at Sister Pauline and Brother Jessie it looks like they are catching up on old times.

GM Mattie looked over at them and said well I have been praying for them to get back together, this would be a good time for them to do so. Yes it would, you know God does works miracles. Sister Ida Mae said. Yes he does, yes he does Sister Mattie said.

Tina walks over to talk to Grandma Mattie and she says out loud, are you alright Grandma Mattie? She replied and said, I'm alright Tina I was just a little surprised today when I found out that Mr. Washington was Pastor Washington. Why it nearly took my breath.

I know what you mean Grandma Mattie, I think that it threw all of us into a loop, why I don't think that none of us seen that coming. Tina said.

Grandma Mattie then thought back to the day that she had mention something to Tina about Mr. Washington. Then she said, you remember when I said that there was some kind of Spirit that I was feeling being around him. Yes I remember Grandma Mattie.

Grandma Mattie then said well this is what I was talking about. He seemed to be a little different than your Pa, Pa. I could just feel it in my spirit. You see one spirit usual recognize another one.

While Tina was eating she stopped long enough to say I see; so Grandma Mattie, are you going to be alright with him being a Pastor of a church.

Well only time will tell Tina, as the old saying goes. There is a first time for everything. She replied. Good, now that's the Spirit to have Grandma Mattie. Then she asked her if she could get her something to drink or eat. She said no I'm fine right now. Ok, she said.

GM Mattie just remembered that she needed to say something again to Tina about how nice Jessie looked. Oh, and I wanted to tell you that I'm glad that you were able to get Jessie to come today. And he looks so nice.

Yes he does she said, I told you that I would take care of him and make sure that he would be there. Yes you did she replied and it looks like Jessie and Sister Pauline are trying to catch up on some things.

Tina looked over at them and said yes it does, you know it would be good if they could get back together again. Grandma Mattie turned and looked back at Tina and said; I know what you mean. I've been praying on that, and I know that God is going to answer my prayers.

Tina laughed and said maybe sooner than you think, here comes Uncle Jessie and Aunt Pauline now.

Uncle Jessie and Aunt Pauline were walking toward her Grandma Mattie smiling and holding hands. Uncle Jessie bends down and hugs Grandma Mattie and so does Aunt Pauline then they take their seats on the couch and started talking to her; the twin sisters had gotten up to go into the kitchen. As he began to talk she was surprised in what all Jessie was telling her.

Uncle Jessie said Mom's I wanted to tell you that I'm sorry for the way that I've been acting. And that I'm glad that I came to church today. Grandma Mattie looked at him with a great big smile on her face and said, and I was glad to see you there too Jessie.

He then said I know that you don't think much of me for the way that I've been acting, but I just wanted you to know that I have been praying and I'm really trying to make some changes in my life. Grandma Mattie was so glad to hear her son Jessie talking like this. It just made her feel so happy for him and Pauline.

And I wanted to also tell you that Pauline and I have decided to get married again. Grandma Mattie couldn't hold her composure; she starting crying and saying; Praise the Lord, Praise the Lord, I knew that it was going to happen. Thank You Jesus for what you have done.

Pauline then looked over at Grandma Mattie and said, and we are going back to my hometown in South Carolina for the Wedding and renew our vows. By this time the whole room had gotten quite. They all begin to say congratulations to the both of them.

Grandma Mattie was so happy she couldn't be still. She looked at the both of them and said, that sounds nice, so let me get with Tina on the arrangements and I guess that we all will be going to South Carolina for the Wedding.

By this time the twins had entered back into the living room and one of them was standing by the couch and the other one sat back down in the chair. Pauline smiled and said that sounds good Grandma Mattie. Then she hugged Sister Pauline and Jessie.

Grandma Mattie then spoke up and said listen up everybody I know that you all have heard the great news that's going on with Jessie and Pauline and I've talked to Tina about us getting a bus and we are all going to South Carolina for the wedding. So get ready cause we all are going to the Beach.

They all were rejoicing with happiness when Sister Hattie Mae spoke up and said really now, can we go too?

Grandma Mattie turned around and looked at Sister Hattie Mae and said why not you come to everything else. Then she continued talking about the plans for the trip. Grandma Mattie wasn't trying to be smart she was just a Sister that was well spoken and she just always told it like she seen it.

Tina started thinking about how nice it would be if Mr. Washington could go on the trip with us. So she looked over at her and said Grandma Mattie, what about Pastor Washington, are you going to ask him to go with you on this trip.

Grand Mattie spoke up and said Tina I'm already a step ahead of you, he said that he wanted to take me to the Beach and this is going to work out real good. I can't wait to call him and tell him the good news.

Tina was smiling and looking at Grandma Mattie she had a glow on her face that made her face lighten up. She knew that Grandma Mattie was full of joy and she couldn't wait to see what Mr. Washington was going to say about going on the trip with them.

This story is the continuation on a grandmother and her success in getting her man Mr. Washington and also on her and her family being invited to come to Mr. Washington church to help him celebrate the pastor Anniversary. And you should be curious to know who Sister Hattie Mae is; she has some interesting information for Grandma Mattie.

Sarah Tuck who is the Author plays the role of Sister Hattie Mae; she is the Author of this book and she is the Writer, Producer, Director and Actor of her own production company called Sarah Tuck Production. In this company is where this story has also been produced as a play.

Betty Britton is playing the role of Grandma Mattie in this story. She is a Writer, Producer, Director, Actor, Sign Language (Beginner -ASL), Computer Oriented of her own production company. She also does Photography and Wedding planning. Betty has also been on television in "Noah Knows Best, HBO Comedy Special w/Jeff Foxworthy & Bill Engvall and Channel Five New Documentary."

Silvia Scott plays the role of Ida Mae in this story and play as one of the twin sisters. She is a minister and she is a Godly women, Praised Worshipper, Mother, Grandmother, Aunt, and Friend. She is originally from Gary, Indiana and went to Horace Mann School and now she resides in Gallatin, Tennessee. She is a widowed and she loves and cares for her family

Evangelist Deborah Alston is a retired North Carolina firefighter, who plays Aunt Pauline in this story and play as Uncle Jessie wife. In 1997 she was directed by the hand of God to move to Nashville, Tn. She was called into ministry as an evangelist and was ordained in 2000. She is an Assisting Minister, Women Prison/Jail Coordinator at First Baptist Church in Gallatin, Tn. She is also the Founder of Deliverance Music Ministry, where she ministers the Word of God in song. Evangelist Deborah Alston Barr is married to Mr. Terry Barr.

Terry Barr is a native of Sumner County, Tn. were he attended Sumner County Schools and Tennessee State University. He's role was played as one of the Deacons in this story named Deacon Beasley and he played Uncle Jessie. He retired from DuPont, but keeps busy in active works in a part-time position for the Sumner County School systems in Gallatin, Tn. He has one son and five grandchildren. He is an active member of First Baptist Church at 290 East Winchester Street, Gallatin, Tn.

ABOUT THE AUTHOR

Contact information

Email: tuckproductions@yahoo.com

facebook.com/protecting2014

twitter.com/sarah1057rabbit

instagram.com/sarah_tuck_production2014